THE MAGNIFICENT
MAKERS

THE MIGHTY MAGNET

Ben Humeniuk

PowerKiDS
press™

New York

To Dad and to John Murray, who both know a thing or two about the weight of responsibility and mentorship.

*Special thanks to Kevin Nuut, who showed me a way to color that
absolutely expedites the process of making these books.*

*And likewise to the Westers, for the generous use of their dining room
as a retreat space. I'm sorry for stealing a few of your mints while I drew the first half of the book.*

Published in 2020 by The Rosen Publishing Group, Inc.
29 East 21st Street, New York, NY 10010

First Edition

Illustrator: Ben Humeniuk
Editor: Greg Roza

Names: Humeniuk, Ben.
Title: The mighty magnet / Ben Humeniuk.
Description: New York : PowerKids Press, 2020. | Series: Magnificent makers
Identifiers: ISBN 9781725307384 (pbk.) | ISBN 9781725307315 (library bound) | ISBN 9781725307438 (6pack)
Subjects: LCSH: Responsibility–Juvenile fiction. | Magnets–Juvenile fiction. | School–Juvenile fiction. | After-school programs–Juvenile fiction.
Classification: LCC PZ7.H866 Mi 2020 | DDC [F]–dc23

Manufactured in the United States of America

CPSIA Compliance Information: Batch CSPK19. For Further Information contact Rosen Publishing, New York, New York at 1-800-237-9932.

CONTENTS

MONDAY MORNING

G.W. CARVER HIGH SCHOOL

CLIK

WHIRRR

SIP

SPEW

4

THE LIBRARY

YES, MR. JENSEN--THEY'RE CALLED MEMES. THEY'RE LIKE, INTERNET JOKES.

MR. BAXTER
(LIBRARIAN/MEDIA TECHNOLOGIST/
MAKER CLUB ADVISER)

YES, WE'RE WORKING ON IT.

DO I... DO I KNOW WHO'S RESPONSIBLE?

RING RING

MR. BAXTER. MR. BAXTER!

I TRIED CONTROL-ALT-DELETE, BUT IT'S NOT WORKING...

BAXTER, I'VE GOT CLASS IN FIVE MINUTES--

FELIX!!!

HEY, MR. BAXTER. WHAT'S UP?

FELIX
(LEAD PROGRAMMER)

FELIX, I'M GETTING A LOT OF ANGRY TEACHERS HERE. WHAT EXACTLY ARE YOU DOING ON THE MAKERS' COMPUTER?

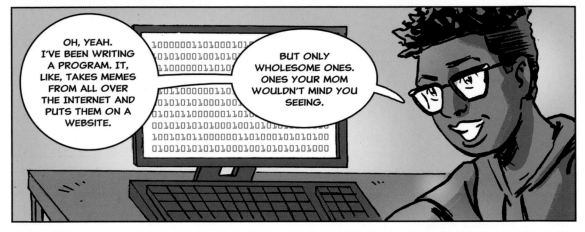

OH, YEAH. I'VE BEEN WRITING A PROGRAM. IT, LIKE, TAKES MEMES FROM ALL OVER THE INTERNET AND PUTS THEM ON A WEBSITE.

BUT ONLY WHOLESOME ONES. ONES YOUR MOM WOULDN'T MIND YOU SEEING.

YOU'RE TESTING THIS PROGRAM RIGHT NOW?

YUP.

USING THE SCHOOL'S SERVER?

UM... YUP?

SHUT. IT. DOWN.

WELL, I TALKED TO DR. DEESEN. I GET TO KEEP MY JOB, AND YOU GET TO STAY ON CAMPUS.

BUT BOTH OF THOSE ARE WITH A "BARELY."

WHAT EXACTLY WERE YOU THINKING BACK THERE?

I'M SORRY. I JUST... I'VE REALLY BEEN THINKING ABOUT THE FUTURE LATELY.

I KIND OF WANT TO BE A PROGRAMMER, AND I FIGURED THIS WOULD BE A GOOD WAY TO TRY THINGS OUT.

THAT... I CAN UNDERSTAND.

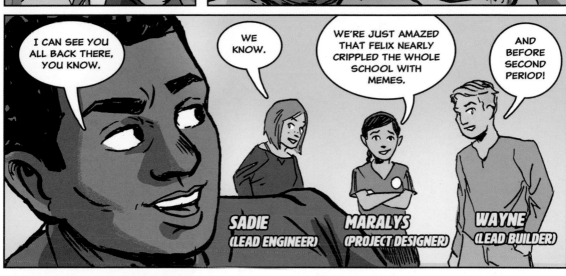

SADIE
(LEAD ENGINEER)

MARALYS
(PROJECT DESIGNER)

WAYNE
(LEAD BUILDER)

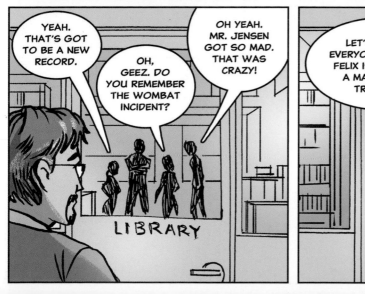

THAT NIGHT

KNOCK KNOCK!

SOME DAY, HUH?

HEY, MICHAEL. SO MOM TOLD YOU?

SHE DOESN'T SNITCH. BUT HER FACE SAID EVERYTHING.

WHAT'D YOU DO THIS TIME?

I GOT BANNED FROM EVERYTHING GOOD IN LIFE, BASICALLY.

I KNOW A THING OR TWO ABOUT THAT. YOU WERE THERE FOR MY SOPHOMORE YEAR, REMEMBER? I WAS WILDIN' OUT...

14

15

AND SO

WHAT HAPPENED TO YOU GUYS?

WE NEED HELP.

YOU NEED A TOWEL.

WE'D SETTLE FOR BOTH.

LOOK, I KNOW I'M ALREADY IN THE DOGHOUSE. I JUST... LOST THIS RING MY BROTHER GAVE ME... AND I WAS HOPING I COULD USE THE COMPUTER TO LOOK UP HOW POOL DRAINS WORK.

18

I CAN'T GET THE LID OFF WITHOUT A CUSTODIAN, AND HE'S OFF CLEANING UP, LIKE, SOME BARF IN THE GIRLS' BATHROOM, SO THIS IS PRETTY MUCH ON ME NOW.

20

THE IDEA IS THAT IF YOU CAN SEND ELECTRIC CURRENT THROUGH SOMETHING LIKE IRON, IT'LL CREATE A STRONG MAGNETIC FIELD, STRONGER THAN A REFRIGERATOR MAGNET.

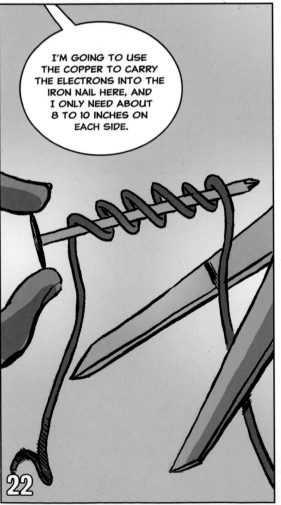

I'M GOING TO USE THE COPPER TO CARRY THE ELECTRONS INTO THE IRON NAIL HERE, AND I ONLY NEED ABOUT 8 TO 10 INCHES ON EACH SIDE.

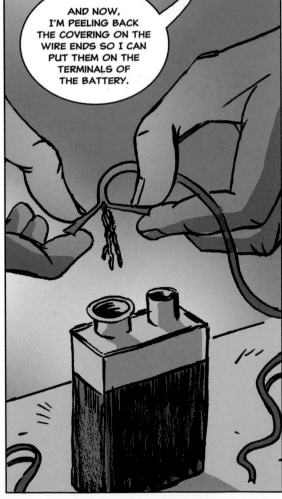

AND NOW, I'M PEELING BACK THE COVERING ON THE WIRE ENDS SO I CAN PUT THEM ON THE TERMINALS OF THE BATTERY.

23

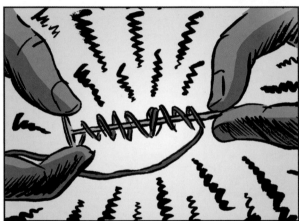

24

TINK!

THAT EVENING

HEY, MICHAEL.

I NEED TO RETURN SOMETHING TO YOU.

BRO, YOU SURE? IT'S ONLY BEEN A DAY.

26

27

29